DEMCO

SNOWBOARD
TWIST

OUTDOOR ADVENTURES

Jean Craighead George

SNOWBOARD TWIST

Wendell Minor

KATHERINE TEGEN BOOKS

An Imprint of HarperCollinsPublishers

Snow fell quietly on the Teton Mountains one night in early December. At dawn it stopped. A layer of new snow had fallen on top of the many older layers.

When the alpine glow of morning colored the mountain peaks pink, adventure-loving Axel stepped outside his family's mountain cabin.

"The perfect snow," he observed. "Time to go snowboarding."

Dag, his father, who was the head of the Teton Rock Climbing School and a snow patrol officer, joined him.

"Dad," Axel said, "can we go to Glory Bowl?"

Dag studied the landscape. New snow can be dangerous in early December and again in spring when the deeper snow layers are unstable. The jolt from a snowball falling off a rock, or a loud sound, can collapse them. They become sliding boards. The layers on top slide downward and avalanche into the valleys. They thunder and boom.

"First we'll check the bowl for avalanche conditions," Dag said. "If Glory Bowl has any mushy old layers, we'll sound off that snow cannon on the high ridge before the skiers and snowboarders arrive. The noise will avalanche the slope and make it safe."

Axel and Grits, the adventure-loving dog, often helped Dag on avalanche patrol. The two were an unbeatable team. Grits had keen ears. Axel had detective eyes. They followed Dag along firm ridges and across stable snow, listening and watching as they checked the slopes for signs of potential avalanches.

As the sun reached the slopes, Dag and Axel, with Grits in his backpack, climbed a ridge well away from the avalanche zone. They stopped on the top of Glory Bowl. Axel looked down.

"Wow!" he exclaimed. "Fresh snow from here to the bottom. And not even a mouse track to mar it."

"Pretty is as pretty does," said Dag. "Before you track up that new snow, we'll test the layers under it."

Dag plunged his pole deep into the snow as he felt for weak layers. He moved carefully. Axel and Grits followed, looking and listening.

"Safe so far," said Dag.

"And the longer that bright sun shines on the new layer," said Axel, "the sooner it will fuse into one solid, safe block with the lower layers, and the sooner I can snowboard."

Suddenly Grits decided the work was over. He whined to get down and romp in the powder.

"Not yet," said Axel to Grits. "The sun hasn't shone down long enough. You've still got to listen for the *whoompf* that tells us a deep snow layer has collapsed, and I still have to watch for the *crack* that tells us the upper layers are sliding. Then, before the pistol shot sound made by the snow block breaking loose, I yell: *'Avalanche!'* and we stay where we are. Got it, Grits?"

Up the ridge trail came Kelly, Axel's snowboarding rival and captain of the school snowboarding team. She was always bragging to Axel that she could do more perfect grabs and flips than he could.

Kelly looked at Axel with a superior glance. Axel couldn't help himself. He pressed on his snowboard, zoomed out, did a master grab, landed, and then glided as smoothly as an eagle to Kelly's side.

"Hi," he said.

"I can do better than that," Kelly said, and quickly pushed off downhill. She frightened a jay roosting in a bush below her. Its wing dug into the snow. A snowball formed. The snowball rolled downhill, growing bigger and bigger. It fell off a cliff and landed with a thump.

Whoompf, said the mountain.

Grits heard it first. He jumped out of the backpack and rushed at Kelly.

"Go, Grits," Axel shouted as Grits ran to cut her off.

The crack opened. It zipped across the rim of Glory Bowl not thirty feet below Kelly.

Grits took a flying leap and knocked Kelly down.

A sound like a pistol shot rang out. Kelly's eyes widened. She knew what that meant. She did not move.

From the summit a thunderous boom sounded. Dag had set off the snow cannon.

Below them a mammoth slab of snow was sliding down mountain. With a deep cosmic roar it avalanched into the valley. It smashed trees, catapulted rocks into space, and sent clouds of ice crystals into the sky.

Silence. The air cleared. The avalanche was over. Dag rushed to Axel.

"Where's Kelly?" he asked, with fear in his voice. He wiped sweat from his forehead. "We've got to find her. Did she turn on her beeper? Where is she?"

Axel pointed to two snowy heaps coming toward them. One was Kelly. She was snowboarding. The other was Grits. He was leaping and tunneling and wagging his tail. Both were safe.

When the two reached Axel and Dag, Kelly was humble. She glanced down the now-bumpy slope.

"Let's go find a smooth slope where I can write 'Grits is a hero' with my snowboard." She picked up the little dog and hugged him.

"You can't write that," cried Axel.

"I can and I will," Kelly bragged.

Meanwhile the bright sun did its work. It changed the structure of the crystals of the new snow. They fused with the crystals of the lower layers, and the avalanche threat was over for the day.

Axel, Grits, Kelly, and Dag went off to join the skiers and snowboarders. Axel performed grabs and flips. Kelly perfected twists. Dag skied loops down the slope, and Grits leaped and tunneled all the way to the bottom.

That evening, back at Dag's cabin, they waited for Kelly's parents to pick her up. Dag paced the floor.

"I must apologize to you, Kelly," he said. "I set off the avalanche too soon. I thought I saw you with Axel well above the crack."

"Hey," Axel said, "you didn't set off the avalanche. A jay bird did." He smiled at his dad. "I was there when it happened. Kelly scared the bird. Its wing hit the snow, the snow formed a snowball, the snowball rolled, it fell off a cliff with a thump, and the thump collapsed a deep mushy layer—and *whoompf, crack, bang*—avalanche!"

"And Grits knocked me down high above the crack," said Kelly.

Dag's face brightened. He walked to the window, and in the frost on the glass he wrote, "A gold medal for the jays."

Kelly ran to another frosted window.

"Grits is a hero," she wrote, and then smiled at Axel. "Thought I couldn't write it, huh?"

Grits looked up and wagged his tail.

Axel rolled his eyes. "Girls!" he said, and stirred the hot chocolate.

More Outdoor Adventures with Axel

CLIFF HANGER

FIRE STORM

To Sage —J.C.G.

To Charlie Craighead —W.G.M.

Snowboard Twist
Text copyright © 2004 by Julie Productions Inc.
Illustrations copyright © 2004 by Wendell Minor
Printed in the U.S.A.
All rights reserved.
www.harperchildrens.com

Library of Congress Cataloging-in-Publication Data
George, Jean Craighead, date.
Snowboard twist / Jean Craighead George ; Wendell Minor.— 1st ed.
p.   cm. — (Outdoor adventures)
Summary: While Axel, his father, Dag, and his dog, Grits, are testing the snow
in the Teton Mountains' Glory Bowl, Axel and his snowboarding rival, Kelly,
witness an avalanche.
ISBN 0-06-050595-8 — ISBN 0-06-050596-6 (lib. bdg.)
[1. Snowboarding—Fiction. 2. Avalanches—Fiction. 3. Snow—Fiction.
4. Teton Range (Wyo. and Idaho)—Fiction.]
I. Minor, Wendell, ill. II. Title.
PZ7.G2933 Sp 2004
[E]—dc21   2003006227
                                                          CIP
                                                          AC

Typography by Al Cetta
1 2 3 4 5 6 7 8 9 10
❖
First Edition